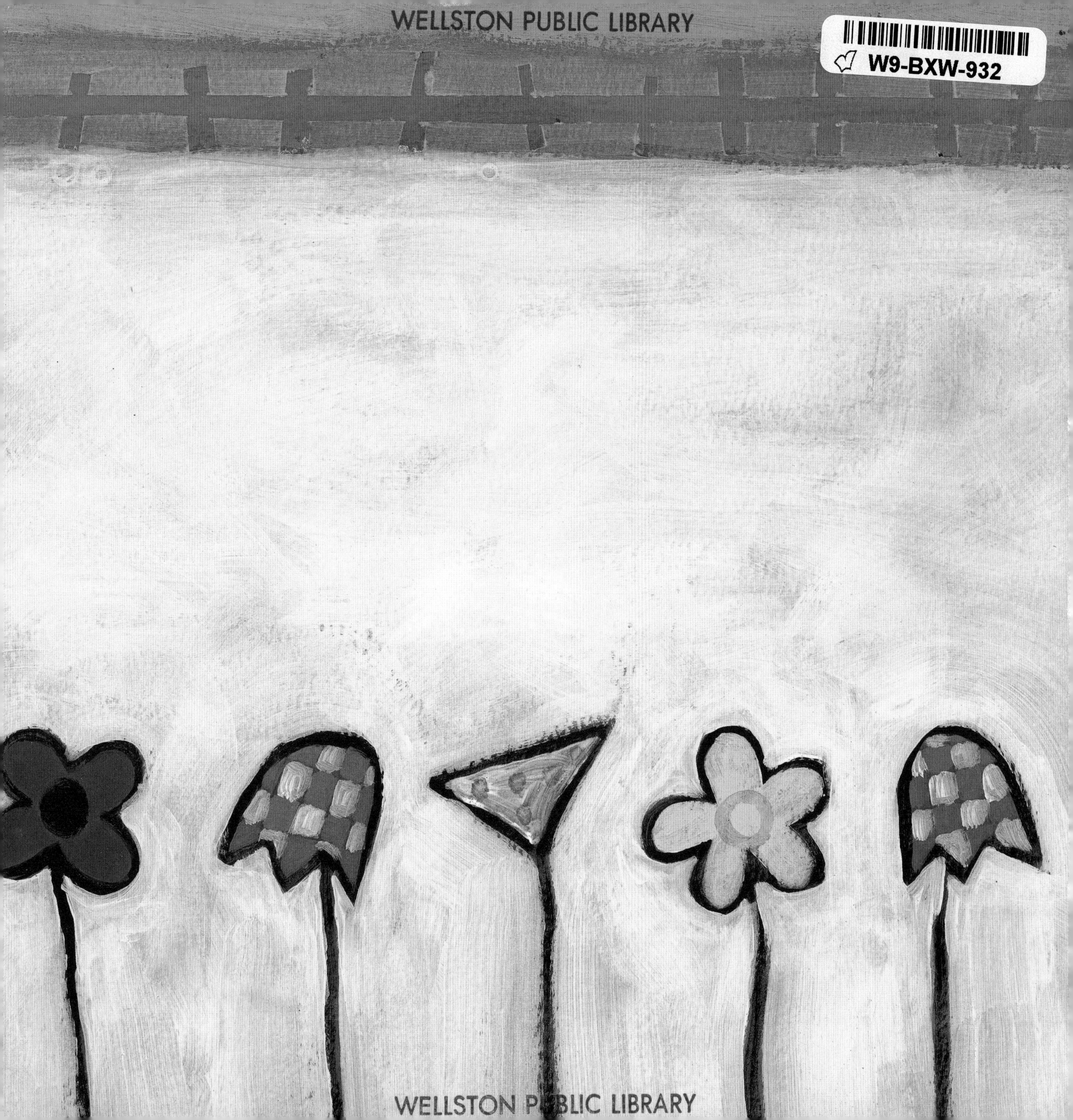

WELLSTON PUBLIC LIBRARY

CLEO THE CAT

Caroline Mockford

walk
the way of wonder...
Barefoot Books

Cleo wakes

Cleo winks

Cleo yawns

Cleo blinks

Cleo needs a friend

Cleo's all alone

Cleo takes a walk

Cleo wants a home

Cleo finds
a house

Cleo
looks
inside

Cleo hears a noise

Cleo tries to hide

Cleo feels hungry

Here's
a bowl
of milk
for you

Cleo's
happy
now

Cleo licks
her paws

Cleo takes a leap

Cleo starts
to purr

Cleo
falls
asleep

For Hannah — S. B.
For Joe — C. M.

Barefoot Books
37 West 17th Street
4th Floor East
New York, New York 10011

This book is printed on 100% acid-free paper
The illustrations were prepared in acrylics on 140lb watercolor paper

Graphic design by Jennie Hoare, England
Typeset in 44pt Providence Sans Bold
Color separation by Bright Arts, Singapore
Printed and bound in Singapore by Tien Wah Press (Pte.) Ltd.

1 3 5 7 9 8 6 4 2

U.S. Cataloging-in-Publication Data (Library of Congress Standards)

Blackstone, Stella.
   Cleo the cat / written by Stella Blackstone ; illustrated by Caroline Mockford.—1st ed.
[24]p. : col. ill. ;   cm.
Summary: Delightful tale of a small cat who explores the world around as she looks for a friend.
ISBN 1-84148-259-5
1. Stories in rhyme. 2. Friendship -- Fiction. 1. Mockford, Caroline, ill. 11. Title.
[E] 21   2000   AC   CIP

walk
the way of wonder...
Barefoot Books

The barefoot child symbolizes the human being
who is in harmony with the natural world and moves
freely across boundaries of many kinds. Barefoot Books
explores this image with a range of high-quality picture
books for children of all ages. We work with artists,
writers, and storytellers from many cultures, focusing on
themes that encourage independence of spirit, promote
understanding and acceptance of different traditions,
and foster a lifelong love of learning.

www.barefoot-books.com